Mog
and the baby

Judith Kerr

Collins

An imprint of HarperCollinsPublishers

For Ben Davis, who is very fond of cats

Mog and the Baby is ideal for children beginning
to read as it uses a limited vocabulary.
Judith Kerr's books about Mog have entertained countless children
for more than twenty years and sold over 2 million copies.

Have you read all these books by Judith Kerr?

Mog the Forgetful Cat
Mog's Bad Thing
Mog and Bunny
Mog in the Dark
Mog on Fox Night
Mog and the Granny
Mog and the Vee-Ee-Tee
Mog's Amazing Birthday Caper

The Tiger Who Came to Tea
The Other Goose
Birdie Halleluyah
How Mrs Monkey Missed the Ark

First published in hardback in Great Britain by William Collins Sons & Co Ltd in 1980
First published in Picture Lions in 1982
Illustrations re-originated for the 1992 edition

17 19 20 18

ISBN: 0 00 664065 6

Picture Lions is an imprint of the Children's Division, part of HarperCollins Publishers Ltd.
Text and illustrations copyright © Kerr-Kneale Productions Ltd 1980
The author/illustrator asserts the moral right to be identified as the author/illustrator of the work
A CIP catalogue record for this title is available from the British Library.
The HarperCollins website address is: www.**fire**and**water**.com

Manufactured in China by Imago

One day Mog was playing with Nicky.

Debbie was going to school.
Mr Thomas was going to work,
but Nicky had a cold.

Mog and Nicky played
Catch the String.

Wa! Wa!

Then they played Bad Dogs.

Then they played Tickle Mog's Tummy,

and then they played ball.

Suddenly they heard a noise.
It was a crying noise.
It was a very loud crying noise.

Mrs Thomas said, "Look who's here.
Mrs Clutterbuck has brought us her baby.
We're going to look after it while she goes shopping."

The baby looked at Mog
and stopped crying.
It said Psss instead.

"It's trying to say puss,"
said Mrs Thomas.

"Will my baby be all
right with your cat?"
said Mrs Clutterbuck.

"Oh yes," said Mrs Thomas. "Mog loves babies."

But Mog and Nicky had to stop playing ball
because the baby did not know how to play.

"I've got a very good idea,"
said Mrs Thomas. "Let's take
the baby for a ride in the pram."

The baby liked riding in the pram.
It said Psss.
"I've got a baby in a pram too," said Nicky.
Mog said nothing, but she was not happy.

When they came back it was lunch time.
But the baby did not want to eat its lunch.
It said Psss instead.

It said Psss and cried.
It cried so much that Mog did not
want to eat her lunch either.

She went away and
sat in her basket.

She sat in her basket
and tried to think of
other things, while
Mrs Thomas and Nicky
cleared the dishes.

The baby found a dish to clear, too.

"Look what it's done," said Nicky.

"Oh dear,"
said Mrs Thomas.
"Perhaps the baby
would like a rest."

But the baby did
not want a rest.
It said Psss Psss Psss.
It said Psss and cried.

"It wants Mog,"
said Mrs Thomas.

"Will Mog be all right
with the baby?" said Nicky.

"Oh yes," said Mrs Thomas. "Mog loves babies."

Mog sat in her basket, and the baby stopped crying.
It was nice and quiet when the baby stopped crying.
It was so quiet that Mog fell asleep.

She had a dream.
It was a lovely dream.
It was a dream about babies.

SUDDENLY ... she woke up.

Mog thought,
this baby is everywhere.

She thought,
I'm getting out.

Mog ran across the road,

but the baby was coming after her,

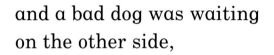
and a bad dog was waiting
on the other side,

and there was a car coming.

"There's my baby!" shouted Mrs Clutterbuck.
"There's Mog!" shouted Debbie.
There's only one way to go,
thought Mog, and she jumped.
She jumped away from the dog.
She jumped away from the car.
She bumped into the baby.
The baby flew through the air
and came down on the pavement.
It said Psss.
Mr Thomas stopped the car just in time.

"My baby! Oh, my baby!" said Mrs Clutterbuck.
"It's a silly baby," said Nicky.
"It shouldn't have run into the road."
"Mog saved it," said Debbie.
"She is a very brave cat," said Nicky.
"She is the bravest cat in the world.   he is a
baby-saving cat, and she should have a reward."

They all went to get Mog a reward.
It was a very big reward.
It was a reward from Mrs Clutterbuck.

"Mog saved my baby from being run over,"
said Mrs Clutterbuck.
"I told you," said Mrs Thomas, "Mog loves babies."